Bob and the Hungry Bunnies

Based on a story by Jimmy Hibbert
Adapted by Dennis Shealy
Illustrated by Barry Goldberg

A GOLDEN BOOK • NEW YORK

Library of Congress Control Number: 2003104371
ISBN: 0-375-82714-5
www.goldenbooks.com
Printed in the United States of America   First Random House Edition 2004
10 9 8 7 6 5 4 3 2 1

It was morning in Bobville, and Bob and his team were hard at work building a "pick-your-own" stand for Farmer Pickles.

"Pick your own what?" Dizzy asked Bob.

"Carrots, cabbages—all kinds of things," Bob explained. "Now people can pick their own vegetables fresh from the field!"

The team loved the idea. Everyone took extra care
with each part of the job—from the foundation to
the frame to the four brick walls. They wanted the
stand to be the best ever!

Later that morning, Spud came running by.

"Hi, everybody! I have a letter for Mr. Ellis. It was delivered to Farmer Pickles by mistake, so I'm taking it to the museum."

Bob and Wendy gave each other worried looks.

"Spud, please take that letter to Mr. Ellis right now," called Bob. "And don't get into any mischief on the way."

"No prob, Bob!" promised Spud. "You missed a spot!"

He laughed as he skipped down the road toward town.

Spud did just as he was told and headed straight
to the museum. But when he got there, the front
door was locked.

"I know!" said Spud. "I'll try the back."

Spud walked inside, leaving the back door open.
He didn't find Mr. Ellis—but there, on a table, were
all of Mr. Ellis' wonderful magic supplies.

"It wouldn't hurt for me to be a magician just for a minute," Spud told himself. He couldn't resist putting on the cape and waving the magic wand!

"Abracadabra!" shouted Spud, knocking over a big, black top hat. Suddenly, Mr. Ellis' bunny popped out of the hat—and hopped right out the open door!

"Come back, Brenda!" cried Spud, chasing after her.
 But it was too late. Brenda had escaped!

Spud found his friends and told them that Brenda had run away. Luckily, Lofty was carrying a giant carrot. It was the wooden sign for Farmer Pickles' stand.

"That's perfect!" Spud shouted. "When Brenda sees this sign, she'll come running! Bunnies love carrots, after all."

Everyone was so busy talking to Spud
that they didn't notice Brenda hopping right by.
She wasn't interested in the carrot—she just wanted
a place to hide from Spud.

"Here, bunny, bunny!" Spud called as he and his
friends searched the countryside. Lofty held the
giant carrot as high as he could.

First one bunny—then two bunnies—then all the wild bunnies in the field saw the giant carrot and hopped right on it.

"Oh, no!" shrieked Lofty. He turned around and headed straight back to town to find Bob.

Bob, Wendy, Mr. Ellis, and Farmer Pickles were having lunch at Mr. Sabatini's pizza parlor when they heard Lofty shouting.

"Help!" Lofty cried. The hungry bunnies were still hot on his heels.

Just then, the bunnies saw the vegetables at the salad bar, which looked a lot tastier than their wooden sign! They hopped right into Mr. Sabatini's pizza shop and started nibbling everything in sight.

"Shoo, shoo!" Mr. Sabatini cried. "Get out of my shop!"

Spud admitted to everyone how careless he'd been at the museum, and that Brenda had escaped. Poor Mr. Ellis was heartbroken.

"We'll find Brenda," Bob assured him. "But first, we have to send *these* bunnies home, and I know just how to do it. Spud, take this big bag of lettuce and start running!"

Later that day, the team completed the farm stand. Up, up went the sign. Farmer Pickles' stand was now open for business!

"Great job!" Bob cheered. Everyone was happy except poor Mr. Ellis. Things had turned out all right for everyone but him.

"I don't know where my Brenda went," Mr. Ellis said sadly. Everyone felt sorry for him—except Dizzy, who was giggling.

"It's not funny," Bob told her.

"Hee-hee, I can't help it," Dizzy said. "Hee-hee, I've had a tickle in my mixer all day!"

"Really?" Bob asked.

Bob reached into Dizzy's mixer, which made her giggle even more.

"Presto!" Bob shouted as he pulled out a fluffy white bunny.

"Brenda!" Mr. Ellis cried, taking her in his arms and giving her a big hug. "You were here all along!"

"I love happy endings," Dizzy said, "but *let us* not forget Spud!"

And the whole team laughed, because . . .

. . . Spud had taken the bag of lettuce and run, as Bob had told him to. As soon as the hungry bunnies had seen Spud, they'd chased him right out of town.

And for all anyone knows—he's still running!